Shackles

By Daniel Maher

SHACKLES

Prologue

As I sit in the somewhat comfortable chair in the room I have been given, I begin to write my story. I look at the scars on my wrists from the punishments of my childhood. I think about what happened and why it happened, which I still don't understand to this day, and I remember the trauma I went through before I turned ten.

Hold on. Sorry. My name is John. I have been told to write down everything I can remember about what happened in my early years and about the people who claimed to be my parents until I turned seventeen. The doctors say doing this will be cathartic, which means it will help me heal. Personally, I don't think it matters too much, and neither does anything else for that matter. I think, maybe after I write this, I will get rid of my pain to the best of my ability. I'm not quite sure what I mean by that. After all, I will be scarred for the rest of my life, both physically and psychologically.

I don't know if I can forgive them for what they have done, and I certainly can't forget all they have done, but what I can do is try to move on.

So here we go. This is how it all went down... (or at least, what I remember of it).

Chapter 1

I guess the best place to start is when I was little and only a young kid. My earliest memories. What I remember from then is that I was always told that the man and woman who raised me were my parents. They always said they loved me, and that they wanted to raise me right.

So when I was four and I wanted to know something, I always asked; I was always a curious little booger. My parents always seemed to encourage my curiosity. They showed love to me then. And they always answered my questions, whatever they were: about stars, people, things that were going on, and sometimes themselves.

I always liked exploring, and we had the greatest place for a little kid to run around. The house my parents had was good sized. It sat in the middle of an immense yard (wonderful for the four-year-old I was) and a had large clump of trees in the northwest corner of the property. There was a small and shallow ravine that ran along the west side of the property. My parents also had a swimming pool. The house was in the middle of a rural area, so we had to drive forty minutes in one direction to get me to preschool.

In preschool, I played with all kids. It didn't matter to me if they were boys or girls. I met some nice kids then, but my two best friends were Hunter and Lily. Hunter had two older brothers and a baby sister whose name was Hanna. Lily was an only child at this point, but she would later get a baby brother. We three musketeers played around and goofed off a lot in preschool. We didn't have a care in the world. We sometimes went over to their houses, but we never went to mine. My parents always seemed to like me going to other kids' houses, but they never wanted anyone else at our house. They always said, "Oh, we live too far for them to come over." Or, "We don't want to inconvenience their moms or dads by making them drive out here." I always went with those excuses, never thinking anything else in my four-year-old brain.

I think my parents started really punishing me when I had an incident with Lily. Lily's parents had a yard full of trees; it was like a jungle in the backyard. Not much grass grew in her yard, and the ground was littered with nifty-looking rocks and sticks. We were playing alone together; Hunter had to go home for the day, and we were running about when Lily's shirt got caught on a tree branch and ripped open. She fell and scraped herself on the rocky ground underneath the trees and started to cry. The shirt didn't get ripped off, but it exposed her front, and she scraped her knees rather badly. So me, not knowing what to do, helped her up and brought her back to the house. Now at that age I knew nothing about the steamier side of life, and I went inside, leaving Lily on one of the porch chairs sitting outside, and ran to get her mother who was the only one home at the time. So, she came outside, and, by this time, Lily was bawling; her mother calmed her down and Lily told her what happened; her mother gave her a new shirt to wear (it had a flower and butterfly on it), and we went back to playing. Her mother didn't say anything other than a thank you to me and went back inside.

A little while later my parents came to pick me up from Lily's house, and her mother complimented me to my parents as they left, telling them, "You're raising that young'un right. He helped Lily back to the house after she hurt herself!" and she laughed a little bit. My mother joined in chuckling and then took me out to the car; upon that, we went home in silence.

When we got home, she had me explain everything that happened. She asked me, "When you saw Lily's chest, did you like that, honey?" I didn't know what that meant, so I asked and she said, "When you're a little older, I'll explain." And that was the end of that.

When my father came home, he gave me four swats with a spoon, and I asked why, and he gave me four more. Then he told me to go to bed for the night.

The next day I went to school and played with Lily and Hunter as usual, and at the end of the day we went to Hunter's house. His house was quaint compared to mine and Lily's, but to a four-year-old me it was amazing. It had several nifty features such as a wrap-around porch, a swimming pool with a slide and diving board, multiple flower beds, and lots of trees around the house. Inside was massive, with five bedrooms on the second floor, a playroom on the third floor, and a den, a kitchen, and an office on the first floor. Us kids always played on the third floor or outside.

We each had our own little "special" game, at which we were the best. Lily was best at running and swimming. Hunter was best at video games and building things. And I was best at board games and hands-on things. While we were at Hunter's house, we would play everything. He had the classic video games, like Build It and SpeedyRacer, and Lily and I could hardly ever beat him. We would play tag and go swimming when it wasn't raining, which Lily enjoyed the most. Sometimes Hunter would lead us in building a fort out of boxes and blankets, which was always fun. We played a child's version of Monopoly and Go Fish; I had a lot of fun because I won most of the time. At times I would lead us in building creative designs with Legos, Marble Works, and Lincoln Logs. We had great times together at Hunter's house, and it was where I always felt the safest. Those were certainly the best times of my life, and never did I think that I would get hurt at Hunter's house. To this day I have never regret going over there.

By playing there that day, I got over my four-swat spanking. There were no further incidents that I can remember through the end of preschool.

During the summer after preschool, I didn't get to see my friends very much. They had their vacations and had to be with older siblings or with parents. That summer was the summer my father started building a room under the house. At the time, I didn't know what it was, but I would soon find out.

That summer, I got swimming lessons and speech therapy to help me talk better. I had a horrible stutter. I couldn't pronounce a variety of sh-, and w- and m-words, and I also slurred my s-es. That summer wasn't very fun, but it helped me develop a lot better and faster than my friends at that age. During the summer, I also explored the trees in my backyard and found some wooden crates in the back of the trees that gave off a putrid scent. I asked my mother what these were. She told my father, and he told me, "Don't you worry about those crates, they're only a fertilizer that I forgot to bury." He glanced at my mother and she said, "Just don't go back out there for a little while, honey."

After that, the summer was uneventful until my dear friends Hunter and

Lily came back for kindergarten. Hunter was five, but Lily and I started as four-year-olds. Lily and I both turned five in September, and Hunter turned five in the previous May. In Kindergarten, we learned to read and write. I developed a love for reading; once I started, I never stopped. Nothing eventful happened in Kindergarten other than I started paying attention to the world around me, and so did my friends.

The following summer, all I wanted to do was play with Hunter and Lily. During that summer, Lily and I would often play together at her house; she always asked me if I wanted to go swimming, and of course I agreed. This is one of the reasons why I always brought a pack of cards, a swimsuit, and a change of clothes whenever I went over to a friend's house. Lily's house was smaller than Hunter's. It was a two-story American frontier-style house with a nice front porch and a wide back porch, with a pool and a clump of trees in the backyard. The inside had four bedrooms and an office on the first floor, with two bathrooms. The upstairs was a big playroom, with a half bath and a storage closet. When Hunter got back from his vacation, we all played together and we did the same things as always until July.

In July, my father finally finished his underground room. He also showed it to me. He told me, "This is where you will be punished if you do wrong, son." I didn't know what to make of this, so I just stared at the room. There were chains and shackles lying around. Multiple belts and tweezers were arrayed neatly on the back wall. There was a place for chains to be tied down on the right wall, and on the left wall was a fireplace.

When my father finally let me go upstairs after showing me the basement, I ran to my bedroom. I had a bed (obviously), a desk, a dresser, a closet, and a tiny window that was almost always shut. At the time, I had a teddy bear I always slept with, so I grabbed it, held it to my chest, and cried. After my little sad-fest, my mother came into my room, and told me, "Don't tell anyone about that room. EVER." I just nodded and hugged my bear.

I eventually fell asleep. The next day, my father was going into town. I wanted to see Lily and Hunter, and my father agreed. When we got to Lily's house, I jumped out, and Lily, who had seen my dad drive up, opened the door and let me in. We played and did our norm. After a while, Hunter came over too, and we just had a good time. I asked my father if I could spend the night at Lily's house, and to my surprise he said yes! He seemed to expect this, as he had a bag and my bear in the back of the car. He gave them to me, and Lily said, "Come on! Let's go play!" and we did. My father drove off, and I was left at Lily's house.

Lily's mother tucked us in bed. We were sleeping on the floor upstairs in the play area, and she went downstairs to go to bed herself. During that night I began having terrible nightmares about that room my father showed me and other things. Just like the monster under the bed, except that I had a feeling darker than just a little thing that would be banished by the light. I woke up and just sat on my pile of blankets for a while, and eventually I fell back asleep.

In the morning, when Lily's mother asked me how I'd slept, I just said, "Good." I was too terrified of my nightmares to say anything about it.

Eventually school started again, and we started first grade. First grade was fun, but when I got home it wasn't. Every day my father would take me down into that basement room and put the shackles on me. I never understood why, and when I asked, I got chained to the wall. I was only in the shackles for a few minutes, but it felt so much longer than that. This continued on throughout the year until Lily noticed the marks on my wrists from the shackles. She asked me, "What are those marks for?"

I said, "I don't know, just don't tell anyone."

When the marks became too apparent, my parents had me stay home for a couple of days and told the school that I was sick. None of my friends thought much of this and neither did I, until my wrists started hurting all the time.

The second semester of first grade I wasn't put in the shackles until the week after school ended, and I was in them for the entire week. In May, Hunter turned seven and invited me and Lily and several other kids from our class to his birthday party. His parents had gotten a raise and rented a bounce house for his birthday. All of us kids bounced and swam until it was time for cake and ice cream, and most importantly, presents!

After the party, everyone but Lily and I went home. We were going to stay for a sleepover and play lots of games through the night. Eventually, we all got tired and fell asleep.

The next day when I woke up, Lily's head was on my chest, and I was stretched out on several cushions, and Hunter had fallen asleep on the couch in his family room. After I got up, Lily woke up. We ate a little breakfast then started poking Hunter awake. We even tickled him a little bit. Eventually Lily had to go home, and I took Hunter aside, and told him, "I don't want to go home, can't I just stay here?"

He looked at me and asked, "Why? Your parents are cool, and you seem to have a nice house."

"I don't know" is all I said.

When my father came back to pick me up, he said, "Son, your mother has something to talk to you about." I asked what it was, and all my father did was reply, "You'll have to wait and see."

My mother told me, "John, sweetie, you and Lily seem to be awfully close," she started out gently, then her voice got a harsher tone in it. "I want you to not screw it up."

"Yes ma'am." That's all I remember saying.

"How long should we shackle him, honey?" she asked my father.

His reply: "I would say about, eh, four days ought to do the trick."

When we got home, my father immediately hit me upside the head and dragged me to the basement where he shackled both of my wrists and ankles to the right wall. He also started a fire. At the time, I didn't know why he had done that, but now I know it was for the heat factor of torture. He stoked it so it would burn for a while, and the room got hot very quickly, and soon, I was dying of thirst. Every so often (now that I'm older, I realize it was every four hours), one of my parents would bring me a small cupful of water. Eventually I had to pee, and the next time my mother came down I told her so. She just chuckled and went up the stairs after giving me my water. Later, I again peed my pants, and I cried because I had done so. I was very embarrassed at myself and felt miserable. My dad would come down every so often and tighten or loosen the shackles, according to his desire, and ignored my needs. I ended up peeing my pants four times during my shackling and crying each time. I eventually got a rash from that experience in some very unfortunate places, but that's better than a burst bladder I suppose.

After the fourth day, I was finally released. I had new, fresh, dark bruises on my wrists, and my parents wouldn't let me go out of the house until they had healed up some. Every day I cried and held my teddy bear because of the pain inflicted, and not just the physical pain but the emotional pain of being locked away from others, especially my friends, for days on end. My parents would let me out of the house that summer just enough to avoid suspicion by the police, my friends, and whoever else might have been concerned about me. My parents knew what they were doing when they punished me; they shackled me and knew how to evade detection. But... everyone slips up eventually, especially humans.

Chapter 2

When second grade started, I had horrible bruises and terrible scars were beginning to form on both of my wrists. My mother made me wear gloves, several bracelets, or paint my wrists black to cover them up. I was told by my parents to not let anyone see my wrists, not even Lily or Hunter. When my classmates asked me why my wrists were black, my typical response was, "I'm just weird" or "I felt like painting myself today." My classmates typically accepted these explanations, and so did my teacher at the beginning of the year. Though toward the end, he started growing suspicious.

My school days didn't change very much other than my friends and I learned more things. School was getting slightly more difficult, and I would spend more and more time at Lily's or Hunter's house whenever I could. Whenever I got home, either directly from school or from a friend's house, my parents would make sure I did my homework. They would then shackle me for hours at a time; occasionally my mother would spank me just because she could. I hated being down in that basement and couldn't wait to get out of it. Every day I would cry with relief when I got out. My parents seemed oblivious to the fact.

My apologies, you must be getting quite bored with this repetition. If you will permit me to add a few more details, I promise I will get to more interesting things about my memory and what happened. I just want to make sure I cover all my bases so you, whoever is reading this, be it doctor, friend, or some snooping person, will understand where this is coming from and why I am the way I am. Now, on with the story...

During second grade, life got a bit more interesting. I hung out with Lily more and more, and we even held hands quite often. She was my first "girlfriend", though at that age one doesn't even have an inkling of what love of that sort is. But it was something that I starved for and craved, as it was something I wasn't shown at home. Now, I didn't lose Hunter as my friend, but with his older siblings being more involved with college and high school, Lily and I didn't get to see him very much. Although we played, talked, and were together as much as we could be.

Now, it so happened that I absentmindedly forgot to paint my left wrist one day. It was in the winter, I remember it must have been, because it was cold, and snow was on the ground. My teacher noticed my wrist. He took a look at it, and felt it gently, and found out it was scarred with a massive bruise. He got angry that someone would hurt me like that, and that someone would even hurt a child like this. He asked me, "What happened to your wrists, John? How did they get like this?"

"I don't know," was my first reply, but he knew I was lying like a rug with that statement. I burst into tears at that, and he hustled me out to the hall so as not to cause a ruckus in the classroom.

Recess was about to start, so he could talk to me for a while should he want to. "Now, let's wash the paint off of your wrist, John. I want to see it."

"Yes, Mr. Hendrickson," I replied. We went to the bathroom, and he helped me wash the paint off. He saw that my right and left wrists had very similar injuries.

He asked, "Who is doing this to you, son? Is it a bully here at school? A sibling or someone close to your family?"

I could tell he was angry and that it wasn't directed at me, but I couldn't bring myself to tell him it was my parents. So I said, "No, sir."

I told him the truth with that statement. I hated lying, and I still hate it. I was taught to always tell the truth unless otherwise told, and my parents didn't want anyone to know what was going on. This was one of those cases which was "unless otherwise told". This was running through my seven-year-old brain as he said, "You can trust me son, I care about you. I want you to be safe and sound. I can't guarantee you happiness, but what I should be able to guarantee is a safe place for you to learn and talk and play. Is that understood?"

"Yes, sir."

"Now tell me, who is doing this to you, and do you know why?"

"I don't know why, sir, and I was told not to tell you by them, and I don't think I should." My eyes started welling up with tears at this.

"Now, now, son, don't cry right now, you're doing well. I understand now." He looked at me very sternly. "Is it your parents? If it is, you need to tell me."

All I could do was nod, because I knew that I would be punished for breaking a rule of my parents. So I started bawling. Mr. Hendrickson let me cry for a few minutes and took me back to the classroom. He then patted my head and gave me a hug. (Nothing inappropriate mind you.) He told me very seriously, "That is very brave what you did, and now I will take care of it. Just leave the situation to me, son. I'll do my best to get you out of it."

"Yes, sir," is all I could say.

Those two words sealed his fate.

For the remainder of the day I couldn't really concentrate on my classwork, which was disappointing because we were reading about bears, and I loved bears. My distraction was noticeable enough that Lily said something to me.

"John, are you okay?" she asked.

"I'm doing just fine." I said, not unkindly. "I just don't feel very well today is all."

"Mm'kay," she said. "Hope you feel better."

"Thanks. Could I spend the night at your house tonight? And your mom could take us to school tomorrow," I said.

She brightened at that. "I'd like that!" she exclaimed. "But I don't know if my mama will like that, or your mama."

"Okay," I said a little disappointedly. I knew by this time my parents would never agree once they found out what I had done that afternoon.

After school ended that day, I asked my mother if I could spend the night at Lily's house. She said no, like most mothers on a school night, and she almost immediately noticed that there was no paint on my wrists and that the bruises were clear for all to see.

"Get in the car!" she yelled. She was very angry, so I promptly flew into that car and she stepped on it home.

On the drive home, my mother grilled me about my day. She soon discovered that Mr. Hendrickson knew what was going on, that I had told him, and that he was going to take care of it. I distinctly remember her saying this, "I won't ever lose you, honey. You're my child, and you won't be taken from me." This both frightened and comforted me.

When we got home, she informed my father of what I had done, and he was furious. He was so furious that it scared me.

He yelled at me, "GET TO THE BASEMENT NOW!"

I scampered as fast as I could downstairs. He then shackled me to the wall with my back to the room and face to the wall. I heard a cabinet opening, then a cracking sound. My father took a whip and started lashing my back with it. "You're seven now, so that means fourteen lashes." He started to swing the whip, and I felt like my back was on fire with the first whip. The next one was worse: it felt as if I was being branded and torn open. After the fourth lash I went numb, and then I lost track of how many lashes. All I know is that I passed out before it ended. I cried out with every one of them, until I no longer felt anything.

That was the turning point for me; I knew now to permanently keep my mouth shut and not tell anyone about anything that was going on. "This is for your own good," my father said. "Why do you force us to have to punish you? We only do this to keep you in the right."

After he was done, he left me shackled for a little while, and my mother came and cleaned me up. The cleaning process hurt like the dickens, many times worse than getting kicked in the groin or some other comparable pain. After I was cleaned, my mother bandaged my back and had me go to bed. That night my back was on fire, and I couldn't sleep for the longest time until I passed out from exhaustion.

My parents didn't make me go to school for the next few days so I could heal up and so that it would not be noticed. I was called in sick, and the story was quite plausible as several of my classmates got sick at that time of year. It was soon before the holiday break that I was back in school. Lily was very happy to see me and hugged me on sight; Hunter made it a point to be around us for the next few days, as he had been going off by himself more and more lately for unknown reasons.

When I got back, during recess again, Mr. Hendrickson asked me, "John, were you really sick, bud? Or did something happen to you?"

"I was sick, sir," I replied. Pain is a powerful teacher, especially to a seven-year-old. "But I'm all better now!" Lily was beckoning for me to come play with her so I said, "May I go play now, sir? My friend wants me over there." I gestured toward Lily.

"Ah, of course. Run along, bud."

I scampered off to Lily and we played games for the duration of the time.

The rest of the year was uneventful until the day before break, when my parents invited Mr. Hendrickson over to our house for dinner and a conference to discuss me. He was going out of town for the break and our farm was on the way out for him, so he agreed. He also was rather wanting to discuss my wrists with my parents and set them straight. I truly believed that he was going to call the cops or social services or some such, or at least threaten with that if my parents didn't stop what they were doing to me.

After school that day, my parents got ready. They locked the basement door; they had me go up to my room. My mother fixed a meal, and my dad did some other things both in the back yard and in the kitchen. I couldn't see quite what, and I didn't know at the time what he was doing.

Eventually the time came for Mr. Hendrickson to arrive, and my father cordially answered the door. He showed him to the living room and they start talking about this and that, and other pointless adult chatter. My mother brought them some of the meal that she made, and also brought some upstairs to where I was. It was one of my favorites: meatloaf, mashed potatoes, and gravy! With the really good sausage gravy that only moms can make. While I was distracted by eating, my father had led Mr. Hendrickson outside, and they started talking about me. The following is what I remember from that conversation.

Mr. Hendrickson got right to the point and was as curt as I have ever heard him be with someone, as he was normally very polite. "Someone has been harming

John, and I would like to know who and why."

"Of course you would like to know," my father said. "I will tell you the truth, it won't matter here shortly. It has been his mother and me. We have been doing it since he was five, and you, sir, have no right or say in how I discipline my child."

Mr. Hendrickson replied, "That is correct, but isn't there a line somewhere? Really? Permanently scarring his wrists? What do you do to him, chain him to a wall?"

"Precisely," came my father's answer.

Mr. Hendrickson got into massive fit of rage at that, "WHY? FOR BEING A KID? WHY NOT JUST SPANK HIM OR SOMETHING OR OTHER THAT NORMAL HUMANS DO?"

"Well, we aren't normal," my dad replied, "and I would ask you to calm yourself down Mr. Hendrickson, or we may have some problems. This is my house, and I don't like anyone yelling or shouting at me on my own property. This is my turf. If we were at your house or office, then I would accept it, but we aren't, so lower the volume." My father's voice got low and dangerous at the last few words.

Mr. Hendrickson nodded, and very angrily but more controlled now he continued. "Answer the question, Mr. Kesherton."

"The answer is irrelevant to you now, Mr. Hendrickson, as I think you won't care about this conversation in about another minute or so."

"Why do you say that?" Mr. Hendrickson asked.

"I made some poison, and my wife laced your dinner with it. My apologies for such a low blow, but we can't have you tell what you know to anyone else. After all, the wife and I don't want to get into any trouble," my father said rather mischievously. "Now if you would, just...die!"

Mr. Hendrickson immediately began coughing and spluttering. I can only imagine what he looked like as he stood there and fell to the ground still coughing, beginning to choke on himself.

"My apologies, Mr. Hendrickson, but you know far too much about this situation now for us to let you go."

I then heard a squishing sound and then a terrifying silence.

I heard a dragging sound, a few grunts, then the garage door opening. From the garage came the sound of electrical tools at work, and then an even deadlier silence. I was too scared to move for a long time, but then I plucked up my courage and took my plate to the kitchen and put it in the sink. While I was there, I saw through the kitchen window my dad coming back from the backyard covered in blood, ever so calm. That scared me more than his previous fit of rage. I ran to my room and stayed there until I fell asleep.

The next morning when I woke up, the fire in the living room was burning cheerfully. I went to the kitchen and poured myself a bowl of cereal. My father came out of his bedroom and looked at me and said, "Did you sleep well, son?"

"Yes, sir," I replied. I was still terrified of how he had been so calm after whatever he had done in the backyard. "Did you and Mr. Hendrickson have a nice discussion?" I asked tentatively.

My father replied calmly, "I would say we did."

"Where did Mr. Hendrickson go?" I asked even more tentatively.

"He left and went on his merry way, and now I do believe that's enough questions about Mr. Hendrickson, son. Why don't we start getting ready for Christmas?"

"Yay! Christmas!" I exclaimed. That drove all thought of Mr. Hendrickson out of my mind, and that year Christmas seemed extra good and fun. We had a lovely time and celebration. With the new year and the return to second grade, Mr. Hendrickson wasn't there. Instead there was a substitute for the rest of the year. The class later learned that he had disappeared, and nobody knew whether he was alive or dead, or where he had gone. With that, other than every three weeks or so being shackled in the basement, and every six weeks getting fourteen lashes with the whip, it was a rather uneventful second half of second grade.

During that summer, I was locked up the first three weeks in the basement, shackled and whipped repeatedly. Naturally, as a kid, I hated being locked up, but I found that the pain and everything else was inevitable. I had become resigned to the pain by now. But something I noticed was that I began building a tolerance to the pain, so that when later pain was inflicted, it took a lot more to actually hurt me.

This became my norm. Every day I came to expect the pain and torture of that horrible, terrible room. After I had endured that, I was finally able to spend the night at Lily's house and not get hurt anymore. To this day, I still don't know how she didn't notice my wrists or ankles when she saw them. With that, a rather typical summer for me, Lily, and Hunter. Then we started third grade, about which there isn't much to tell, or the remainder of elementary school. I wrote down just what was most vivid in my mind at the time, and still is now. But then middle school, a whole new ball game. One that wasn't very nice to me, I feel like, but isn't that how it goes with anyone and everyone in middle school?

Chapter 3

Middle school: probably the hardest time in anyone's life, except maybe high school, but of the two, I would say middle school is tougher. Not because of classwork or school functions and expectations. But for something much deeper that everyone has to deal with: emotional development. A very painful process, and one that I detested throughout middle school. I began acting out in middle school: hitting others, shouting at random times, crying at weird times. It was really incredible that I had kept Lily and Hunter as my friends, but they were amazing friends.

I now know that it was the shackling to the wall that made me act out that way. My parents never found out that I was acting out, and my peers just thought of me as strange. The teachers and principals also thought it was only pre-teen angst. Which I'm just glad that my parents never found out; I can only imagine what they would have done if they did. But there was one day that started the downward spiral of my mental health.

I was already becoming unstable. There were early signs of it, but they could be passed off as "growing up" or something along that line of reasoning.

But the day started out with my father hitting me three times with a whip to wake me up. I woke immediately and started to cry from pain and surprise. My mother had made me breakfast of scrambled eggs, bacon, and milk to drink. My back was bleeding the whole way to school, and it felt as if it was on fire. I could barely concentrate through the day, and it was the last hour of the day when my teacher noticed that I had dark splotches across my back.

Neither of my friends had noticed it, or if they had they didn't say anything, figuring it was just part of the shirt. But, as it turns out, my back had opened during the day and I had bled quite a bit for a little while.

My teacher, Ms. Reid, said something to me about it, and all I remember is nodding and saying it was nothing. Ms. Reid was a kind, older lady. She was wrinkled and had wispy gray hair. She was also very fond of kids and loved teaching. As far as I know, she had been teaching forever. But really it was something around thirty-four years. She was much harder to fool and get off my back than I thought she would be. I wouldn't tell her a thing, because after all, pain is a powerful teacher.

When my mother came to pick me up, Ms. Reid said to her, "You might want to check on John's back, the back of his shirt is quite splotchy. I think it might be blood."

"I'll look into it," my mother said, with a note of concern in her voice. Though she knew quite well what it was and wasn't concerned one bit, at least not about my back. Ms. Reid was likely more on her mind.

That was when I began to dislike my parents. Especially my mother. She could put a stop to my pain, but she didn't. She let it continue and encouraged it! How I began to hate her! But I still had to listen. I had nowhere to turn. My friends would have happily helped me, but their parents would not. After all, what is the word of a sixth grader to that of an adult? I thought back to Mr. Hendrickson. How could I possibly subject my friends to the same punishment? No one believes kids. Kids are too prone to lie or make stuff up. But how I wished for

an escape! How I wished for the pain to end!
I remember these thoughts going through
my head, and they still do today.

I grew angry. I refused to get in the
car and ran inside the school to the boys'
bathroom. I knew my mother would be
furious for my defiant behavior, but I began
to no longer care. Ms. Reid eventually found
me and got me to go home with my mother.

My mother scolded me there.
"Why'd you do that?" she asked.

"I don't know," was all I said.
Though I perfectly knew, I couldn't say
anything there in front of Ms. Reid or my
peers that were still there.

My mother berated me on the way
home, and she yelled at me for letting my
back open up and bleed as it had. When we
got home, she informed my father, who
immediately took me downstairs, shackled
me to the wall, and whipped my back to

shreds. Then he lashed my stomach a few times just to get the point across. The day was a Friday, and I will never forget the pain I experienced on that day; I wouldn't wish it on anyone. Over that weekend, I healed up a little, enough so that I could go to school on Monday. But when my father woke me up, he covered my back with bandages; so, that way, if my back bled it wouldn't be noticeable.

Ms. Reid asked me on Tuesday what had happened to my back, and I told her, "While I was playing in my backyard, I climbed a tree and accidently fell a ways, and the branches sliced across my back, making it bleed."

It was an entirely plausible explanation, but it was a total lie all the same. Ms. Reid seemed to know it was a lie but accepted the story as it stood. Though I think she began suspecting something then.

Nothing eventful happened for some time, other than more shackling to a wall, and alcohol being poured on my back to clean it. To this day, I really don't know which felt worse: the actual whipping or the cleaning process. Both were torture.

But there was an unfortunate day that when I was stretching in class, my shirt came up and Lily saw the faint marks of the previous whipping on my stomach. "What happened to your stomach?" she asked.

All I could think of to say was, "Oh, just some branches in my backyard whipped me across the stomach while I was running through them."

She bought the explanation and returned to her work. I felt horrible for lying to my best friend, but I guess it was necessary at the time. I didn't want any trouble. I didn't want to get hurt more. And I didn't want to drag her into my pain. So, I just dealt with it. Unfortunately, Ms. Reid overheard her and held me back a few minutes after school.

She told me, "I don't believe that branches made those marks across your stomach, and if you would please, show them to me."

She said this so seriously that I did without question. She gently felt the marks and said, "These weren't made by any branches. These are whipping marks! Now, honey, who whipped you? This is not all right. This is very serious and could be child abuse. I need to know so I can help you."

"It was branches! I swear it was branches, Ms. Reid. Nobody whipped me," I said frantically and burst into tears.

As conciliatory and nice as she could be Ms. Reid said, "Please do not lie to me." She noticed the bandages on my back.

"What are these for?" she asked mid-sentence.

"For the wounds on my back that were there last week." I said.

"Hmm..." she mused. "Would you mind if I took several off to see what your wounds look like?" she asked in a tone that brooked no argument.

I nodded. She then gently peeled off a few of the bandages and saw to her horror that my back was still in shreds and welted. "Oh my goodness gracious!" she exclaimed. "Who would do this to you, sweetie? Much less who would do this to a child?"

"A very sick and twisted person," I said back with a tone of bitterness. "I'm sorry, but I can't tell you who did it. I'll get in more trouble than I already am." I said, "If you would please put the bandages back, I would greatly appreciate it." I looked at her, "I really need to leave before my mother gets angry at me."

"Of course, sweetheart," she said. She then put the bandages back just as they were before.

"Thank you," I said, and promptly walked away out the door to my mother's car and got in.

"What took you so long to get out here?" my mother asked.

"Ms. Reid was talking to me," I said.

Ms. Reid then came up to the car and tapped on the window before my mother could pull away.

A brief flash of annoyance flashed across her face before rolling down the window and in a cordial tone said, "Yes, Ms. Reid?"

"Well, I believe something is going on with your son," Ms. Reid began.

"Yes, I'm aware of his behavior at school," she interrupted.

"Not that, Mrs. Kesherton. It is several marks on his stomach and a lot on his back that look like whipping marks. And several are bandaged up."

My mother nodded and acted surprised. "Oh no! Those aren't whipping marks; all they are are just branch marks from when he fell from climbing one of the trees in the backyard." She chuckled. "Boys will be boys. Am I right? No matter what you tell them, they're going to do stupid stuff anyway, and this is what happens."

"What about the marks on his stomach?" Ms. Reid asked, not believing a word of it. "He was running through a clump of bushes and the branches smacked him up real good, poor little guy," she answered.

"I don't believe a word of it. There may be some kernel of truth to what you have said, Mrs. Kesherton, but I know child abuse when I see it, and I won't stand for it!" Ms. Reid exclaimed vehemently.

"I don't take kindly to being called a liar or a child abuser!" my mother exclaimed back angrily. "I think you have crossed your bounds there, Ms. Reid!" My mother started rolling up the window.

"I will go to the police if I have to!" Ms. Reid said. "There is no excuse to inflict this kind of pain on a child!"

My mother shouted back, "We'll see about that!"

As we drove away, I heard Ms. Reid say, "I'll be giving you a call this evening!" My mother simply ignored that and drove us home.

When we got home my mother informed my father of all that had happened.

He got furious and sent me to my room. He and my mother talked for a while. Soon the phone rang. My father picked it up and started talking. It turned out to be Ms. Reid, and she wanted to schedule a meeting with my father and mother to discuss the wounds on my stomach and back. He agreed, and they set up a time to meet at Ms. Reid's home.

After this he came to my room. He asked me rather calmly, "Why did you show her your stomach and back?"

"I didn't have a choice!" I shouted. "Lily saw my stomach when I stretched in class, and I told her it was branches. Ms. Reid overheard and didn't believe me!" I started frantically. "After school, Ms. Reid had me show her my stomach and she noticed the bandages on my back! She didn't really give me a choice in the matter!"

"I understand, son. I will take care of it." He said this very calmly. I was terrified of what he was going to do, but I didn't dare say anything. All I did was nod. "Now, I have a meeting with her at her home on Friday. You will stay here," he said.

"Will I be in the shackles?" I asked.

"I have yet to decide that," he replied.

My mother walked into the room, and asked him, "What are we going to do about Ms. Reid?"

"Well I was hoping we could avoid any further unpleasant business," he answered, "but I guess we have no choice." He gave a meaningful glance to my mother, and soon they both left the room.

I dreaded the oncoming weekend, and I was so scared of it that the week seemed to fly by much faster than it should have. But Friday came, my mother picked me up, and she took me home. She shackled me to the wall in the basement immediately as we walked in the door. "Now when your father gets home, we may let you out of those. Until then, think about how you will handle future interactions with your teachers, and what you will allow them to see and not to see. No one has the right to lift your shirt up, or to ask you to other than your parents. Am I clear?"

"Yes ma'am," I said. Though at that I so desperately wanted to shout, rage, rant, and scream at her with all my fury. I wanted her to feel the pain that I was feeling. I wanted to inflict as much pain as I could. But I wasn't strong enough to break out of the shackles, and I knew it would be futile to try. So, I just hung there defeated and angry, and because I didn't know how to express these emotions, I cried. I cried like a little baby, and I felt like one too.

Meanwhile, after school, Ms. Reid had gone home, and she got ready for my parents to come visit her. My parents soon left, and I was left in the shackles for a long time. I soiled myself while they were gone, and I got upset at myself for that; and, I wondered a way out of my predicament but couldn't find any.

A few days later, I overheard my parents discussing what they had done to Ms. Reid. I pieced it together and it went something like this: After they had shackled me to the wall, my father had gone to the kitchen and gotten a butcher's knife, then they left and locked up the house. They took my father's car into town and met Ms. Reid at her place of residence. She let them in, and they went to go sit in her living room. My mother, while her back was turned, hit her really hard on the head, knocking her out instantly. They both took Ms. Reid to the car as fast as they could, and they propped her up as if she had had a heart attack or stroke. So that way, if anyone saw them, they could plausibly say they were taking her to the hospital. So, they got in the car and drove in the opposite direction of the farm and eventually got to a river. There my father got out of the car, got a tarpaulin out and laid it neatly on the ground, and threw Ms. Reid, who had by this time come to, out of the car and onto the tarpaulin. He first started brutally stabbing her chest and stomach, making a horrible bloody mess everywhere. After he was done with stabbing her, he ripped out several of her teeth and broke several others. He then proceeded to gouge out her eyes and beat her head with the handle of his knife. After this was done, he shaved off the tips of her fingers and toes. Then finally after he had finished removing all forms of identification he could think of, he dumped her in the river where, ideally, she would be washed away.

He then proceeded to clean up his mess, meticulous so that no evidence would be left except a small indentation in the ground. He got into the car with my mother and they drove back to Ms. Reid's home and got her car, locked her house up, and drove off with it. They later dumped the car in an empty abandoned field forty miles out of town, and then they came home.

When they came home, my father went to the bathroom to clean up, then he went to the backyard and buried the tarpaulin. My mother came downstairs and unshackled me. I rubbed my wrists and said nothing. I just went to my room and went to sleep.

During the weekend, I wasn't shackled, but I wasn't allowed out of the house until Monday. When Monday came, there was a substitute in Ms. Reid's place. The story was that she and her car hadn't been found yet, so no one knew anything, but the police were investigating this.

Two officers came to our class and asked if anything strange had happened with Ms. Reid, and there were a variety of answers. A mixture of actual no's and some bull answers as well. The typical sixth grader responses. The police didn't suspect me or even look at me twice in their investigation. They did however interview other teachers, the principal, and her neighbors. Unfortunately, no one had seen anything, and the police stopped interviews but kept looking for her and her vehicle.

Several days later, the police found her vehicle in the abandoned field that my parents had left it in and began a very intense investigation around it. They didn't find any fingerprints other than Ms. Reid's, and nothing seemed out of the ordinary. The police discovered that a tire was flat, and the car must have rolled off the road when she had tried to stop. That would explain how it ended up there, but not where she had gone. The dogs couldn't find any scent there, the scene was too far gone. The police had a cold case, much to the relief and benefit of my parents.

I knew that my parents were killers, but past experience told me that any rebellion against them was futile. And who would have believed me anyway? No one in the town of Aslo, that's for sure. After all, what is the word of a kid against an adult? Especially an "emotionally disturbed" kid. I know I should have said something, anything. My fear was too powerful. Pain is a very powerful teacher.

That was essentially the only remarkable thing in sixth grade, but life for

me got a little bit more bearable in seventh
and eighth grade

*I hear a sound behind me, and I turn and see
Lily standing there. "We need to get out of
here," she says. "I know," I reply, "but first
let me finish what has led us to come this
far, and then we can go, okay? I need just a
few more hours. The doctors said writing
this out would help, and to my surprise it
is!"*
*"I have learned something you should
know," she says very seriously.*
*"I'm sorry, Lily," I begin. "But let me finish
this first, then I will give you my undivided
attention. All right?"*
*"All right," she says, and comes and sits
next to me. "Where ya at?"*
*"Just finished with sixth grade and Ms.
Reid's death," I reply.*

*"Well that's farther along than I am, I'm
still in second grade!"*

*"Well, I can't wait to read your perspective,
Lily, but I really need to finish, otherwise
it's going to bother me."*

*"I understand." She smiles. "I love you."
She then kisses me on the cheek and leaves
the room.*

*For a moment I am stunned, and then I
continue to write.*

Chapter 4

The next phase: seventh grade. One of the best and worst years of my life. The best because I got really close to Lily, and I was over sixth grade. The worst because I acted out more, and my parents inflicted crueler punishments on me. By this time my wrists had become permanently scarred, along with my ankles. They were always hurting, and still do most of the time. Now, on to what happened in seventh grade.

The best place to start, I think, is the day before school started. During the summer I had spent a lot of time at Lily's house. Much more than normal. I wasn't being whipped or shackled there, so I enjoyed it the most. Whenever I was with her, I just felt safe and complete. I wonder if even then I was in love with her, but how can a seventh grader know love? Or really understand it?

Anyway, the day before school started, I was sitting in Lily's house just relaxing and lying on the very comfortable couch, when I started massaging my wrists. Lily then walked into the room, and she started a conversation. This is what I remember, and I made a complete fool of myself, and I regret, very sincerely, how I acted.

"Good morning! How'd you sleep?" she started out.

"Just fine," I replied.

"Are those nightmares still bothering you?" she asked.

"I said I was fine." I raised my voice a little bit.

"O-okay," she said, clearly not believing me. "I just want to make sure you're okay. You wake up screaming every night or crying or begging for mercy, and I hear it. I just want to see if I can help."

"I understand," I said. "But I'm really fine. I'm sorry I yelled. I'm just a little bit nervous about school tomorrow, and I'm rather tired still. I'm not a morning person," I continued. "Someone's rather chipper this morning! Did you rest well? And I'm hungry." I got up to get breakfast for both of us. After staying for two weeks, I had essentially moved in. My parents were going to take me back a week after school started. But until then I enjoyed my time at Lily's and learned how to cook a few things, like eggs.

I began making eggs, and Lily followed me into the kitchen. She said, "I slept well until I heard you crying again, then I fell back asleep. Is your bear not helping anymore? Maybe you should see a doctor?"

"No!" I shouted. "I'm not crazy! And my bear is doing me just fine!"

"I never said you were crazy. I just think that might help, and so does my mother—"

I slammed the pan down and finished the eggs, left them on a plate and stormed out the door. I left in such disarray I was still in my pajamas. It took me a few minutes to realize this, and before I made it back to Lily's house, several people saw me and openly stared, probably thinking I was crazy.

I made my way back and was in tears when I came returned. I profusely apologized to Lily and went to my room and hugged my bear. This was becoming unbearable! How was I going to survive seventh grade when all the people that found out ended up dead, and I couldn't even say anything without it being discounted?

Maybe I should just not continue, but then I thought of Lily and Bear and decided to try seventh grade.

I stayed in my room the rest of the day, and I didn't eat until Lily's mother came into the guest room and gave me a plate of dinner. She said, "I know you're upset, and you are fine. Just eat and you'll feel better. After all, tomorrow is the first day of seventh grade! You'll have fun. Besides, what have you got to lose? Also, if you have more of those nightmares, you just tell them to go away, or this mighty bear," as she held up the bear, "will fight them off!" She chuckled a little bit. "Enjoy your dinner, you're welcome to join us in the dining room when you're ready." Then she left.

I ate the dinner Mrs. Mansfield had brought me. It was delicious. After I finished, I walked out, put my plate away in the sink, and asked if I could go to Hunter's home for a few minutes. Mrs. Mansfield was surprised, and Lily just stared at me.

"I just want to talk with him for a few minutes," I said. "There is something I would like to talk to him about, that I just can't talk to...well…. a lady about."

"Ahhhh. I understand, sweetheart. Let's get going, then, it is almost too late to go," said Mrs. Mansfield.

"I can walk there," I said.

"Nonsense! I'll drive you. Do you want Lily present as well?" she said.

"I think the conversation should be between me and Hunter."

"All right." She then looked at Lily. "Don't worry, honey, we'll come back and it's just probably boy stuff. You can stay home alone if you like."

"Okay," she replied. "But I don't want to stay home. I want to go."

"All right, but I don't think you will be privy to their conversation."

"That's all right. I think I can support John just by being there."

As she went a little red in the face, I realize now that she had a huge crush on me at the time. "I really don't care," I said, rejoining the conversation. "I just really need to talk to Hunter."

Now, I will admit, I had and still have a crush on Lily, and I am possibly in love with her. But she doesn't deserve me. I think the best thing for her to do is to move on from me and try to heal and get herself a real man. Not a weak and scarred one such as myself. Though, I don't think she wants to, not after what we have been through and done together. Anyway, on with the story...

Mrs. Mansfield drove Lily and me the five minutes to Hunter's house. Aslo isn't that big, and there are only five real neighborhoods scattered throughout town. Then there are several outlying houses and farms, such as mine. After arriving at Hunter's house, I got out and ran up to the door. I then knocked, and one of Hunter's siblings answered the door. He looked at me, then he called out for Hunter to come to the door.

Hunter came to the door, a little surprised that I had come. He obviously wasn't expecting to see me until tomorrow. "What do you need?" he asked.

"To talk to you, in private, it's important." I replied.

He stepped out onto the porch, closing the door behind him. "What do you need to talk to me about?" he asked, getting right to the point.

"Well," I began. "I need this to stay between you and me. No one, not even Lily, can know. Okay?"

"All right," he said.

"My parents are horrible people. They are the cause of my wrists hurting all the time, the scars, and the wounds on my back. I hate them! I want this pain to end! I don't want to ever go back home! It's the reason I have nightmares!" I was shouting frantically and manically toward the end.

"Whoa, whoa, whoa...let's just calm down a little bit," he started.

"CALM DOWN!? I DON'T WANT TO CALM DOWN! I'm sorry to have bothered you. I knew you wouldn't believe me. But I didn't want Lily to know…"

"I do believe you," he said. "And I will keep quiet about it. Are you sure you don't want to go to the police about it?"

"I-I'm sure," I said, much calmer now. "I'm sorry for my outburst." I then turned to leave. "See you tomorrow."

"Wait," Hunter said. "Is there anything I can do?"

I replied, "Just keep everyone away from me, and don't let anyone else become involved. I don't want anyone else ending up dead…." I trailed off. Then I clutched my head as it began to hurt. "I-I'll see you tomorrow…." Then I got back to Mrs. Mansfield's car.

"How'd it go, hon?" she asked.

"Well," is all I said.

"What was wrong?" Lily asked.

"Just some boy stuff." I replied. I hated lying to her, but I wanted to ensure that she stayed safe. I wouldn't, and I still won't, ever let harm come to her.

Mrs. Mansfield drove us back, and I then proceeded to get ready for bed, as did Lily.

The next day was the beginning of seventh grade. One of the best years of middle school. Personally, I loved seventh grade. For several reasons. One, I got my first kiss. Two, I got to spend so much more time with Hunter and Lily. Three, I wasn't whipped as much as I had been or later would be. It seemed that this year was a year of respite.

The first days of seventh grade were uneventful, and I don't even remember my teacher's name from that time. All I know is that he never took an interest in me, either as a person or a student. I had several outbursts in his class, one of which I clearly remember.

It started out as a normal day, sometime late in the fall or early winter, and our teacher was giving us a lecture on how important homework was. I clearly remember him saying, "It's for your own good." At which I yelled and flipped over my desk and ran out of the room crying.

I later came back during lunch and apologized and begged him not to call my parents. To which he said, "I'm sorry, John, but your parents must be informed of your misbehavior. I know no one wants to do homework, but it's for your own good. It will make you a better person and throwing a fit over it won't help you. We don't all get our way."

I started shaking with the usage of that horrid phrase again. I couldn't stand it and I didn't know why, so I excused myself and left the room, and didn't come back until the next day to that class.

One other incident in seventh grade that still sticks with me. This one needs a bit

of background for it, so please forgive the
lengthiness of this. So, we will begin from
the very first outburst I had in seventh grade.
This one earlier than the aforementioned
outburst, sometime in the early fall. I don't
remember what caused it, only that I shouted
and disrupted the class. One of my
classmates, who had been in my class since
kindergarten, said, "Oh, not again!" and
other snide comments. He even started
calling me names like "Krazy Kesherton",
"Jaundiced John", and "The Joker". I wasn't
any of those things, but he started rumors
behind my back that I had killed the teachers
that took an interest in my well-being. He
seemed to think that I was crazy and needed
to be locked up.

The incident I am referring to
happened between me and this kid, who I
am intentionally avoiding naming for his
own safety and for his privacy. He has

matured now that he has grown up a bit, and I forgive him for the name calling and such. He wasn't that far from the truth either. Now, to the point. It happened during lunch break or recess (whatever you want to call it). He was talking about my most recent outburst, and he and his friends seemed to think it was funny. Then he got the bright idea to start mimicking it. He then looked over at me and walked over to me and said very loudly, "Well if it isn't the crazy one!" and he started shaking and stuttering like I sometimes did when called on.

"Please stop it," I said quietly.

"I don't think I will," he said. "Actually," and he burst into fake tears and caused a big ruckus, "I-I-I don't want to! Please, no more! Please stop hurting me!" he said in a mocking voice.

I started walking away when everyone else started laughing. Now, Lily wasn't in the courtyard at the time, but Hunter was. When he heard what was going on, he didn't say a word, just shoved this kid hard enough that he hit the ground with an "Ooomphf!"

"Leave him alone!" Hunter shouted. He knew what was actually going on and couldn't put a stop to it, so he tried to help in other ways. He then said, "John has a real problem. And it isn't funny to make fun of it. Do I make fun of you for not having a father?"

The kid then leapt up and punched Hunter in the mouth, who then responded with a kick to the sternum. The bully then responded with another punch that glanced off Hunter's shoulder. Hunter then swung and hit him straight in the nose.

By now the attention of the entire courtyard was on them, and somebody had run to get a teacher or principal, I don't really know. One of this kid's friends then decided to join the fight, so did I. What was a one on one soon became a brawl with a two on two. I landed a few good punches and kicks, as did Hunter.

But before any serious damage could be done, the principal and four teachers showed up. The principal, Mr. Dever, grabbed the kid and pulled him away from Hunter, and another teacher grabbed me, and eventually, order was restored to the courtyard. He brought all of us to his office and had us write down what had happened. He then proceeded to call our parents. This is where things got worse for me in seventh grade. Mr. Dever gave the kid and his friend five-day suspensions, Hunter detention, and me he gave a warning to.

My parents, when they found out that I had gotten into a fight, immediately shackled me to the wall once we got home.

They then brought a new element to my pain
and torture: sound. My father put a stereo
blaring with static or really loud music and
playing it for hours on end. How I hated it!
This was worse than the whipping; I
remember screaming with the sound. But no
one heard me. The music was too loud.
Every day after school this would happen. I
couldn't do anything about it, and the pain
was unbearable. When would it end?

This happened day after day. On the
weekends it lasted for half the day,
approximately twelve hours. I blame nobody
but myself for this, and to this day I can't
stand loud sounds. They set me off faster
than anything else. The doctors tell me this
is an extreme case of hyper phonophobia.
Though, of course, I don't care anymore.

Not much else happened in seventh
grade, except the single best memory I have:
my first kiss with Lily. It wasn't very

special. I arrived at school one day, and she was waiting for me. She told me, "I love you, John. I will always look out for you. You're the one I want." Then she kissed me on the lips and walked away. I was just stunned for a while, and before I could talk to her, she went to class. I didn't get a chance the rest of the day to talk with her, and I didn't know really what I would have said to her either.

Those were the most significant events in seventh grade, and eighth grade wasn't much more eventful. My parents continued with more sound torture and whippings that left my back splayed open. They were long enough that I missed days at a time.

Chapter 5

Now to more recent events: high school. The best time of most people's lives, but not mine. Some parts were good, of course, but most were bad. I really didn't like high school. There was so much drama and immaturity, as well as my parents treating me worse.

I guess the best place to start is freshman year. The high school I went to was Aslo High, named after our "ever glorious town in the great state of Pennsylvania." No, not at all. Curse this town with its naive people! Anyway, freshman year. The worst year of high school. No one cares about the freshman, as well as they should. It's our first year in a whole new world. But there was nothing redeeming about my freshman year except that Hunter and I got really close. After the fight in seventh grade, he started hanging around me more often. He also knew why I was the way I was. I told him everything. He became my confidante, and to this day, I haven't found anyone like him. Not even Lily could be this for me.

During that summer, I was left shackled for four weeks. This was the longest stretch that I had been left shackled. I wasn't unshackled at all in the month of June, and my wrists became permanently scarred. I had very little freedom, and only a bucket to relieve myself in. My mother would come down twice a day with a glass of water and one meal a day, most likely around midday. I really can't say for sure, as I had no way to keep track of time. The last three days were the worst though; my father whipped me repeatedly. My back was just a few strips of skin at the end of it, then my mother cleaned it with alcohol and other painful antibacterial ointments. How I hated them both, but I couldn't do anything. I kept thinking things like, "Kids are powerless compared to the authoritarian structure of society, and worthless in the grand scheme of things. No one cares about us. The only reason to care about children is to take advantage of them. It is very easy to do that. Who defends us? The answer is no one. We are out in the cold, fending for ourselves in a cruel, dark world."

The rest of the summer, once I healed up, I spent at Hunter's house. Lily was out of town for most of the summer; otherwise, I would have spent my time at her place. But during that summer, I got really close to Hunter. He didn't replace Lily by any means, but he still knew, and I told him everything, from my parents abuse to my crush on Lily.

"She has a huge crush on you, y'know," he said.

"She does?" I replied. Surely such a thing could not be true.

"It's so obvious! She's in love with you, dude. One of the hottest girls in town is pining after you! You should ask her out. I'd be willing to bet that she'd say yes."

"Well…I don't know. Why would she want to date me? I'm nothing special."

"You're more special than you know, John. I only wish I could tell you what I found out. But now is not the time, and I was sworn to secrecy."

"What did you find out?" I asked.

"That I can't tell you, friend. I made a promise that I intend to keep, so please do not push me to break it," he said with stubborn pride.

"All right," I said. I knew I could trust him. I knew that he was the most trustworthy person in Aslo, and if he didn't want to say something or had made a promise, come hell or high water he wasn't going to say it or break that promise. He was second only to my creators, whom I could always trust with divine punishment.

Near the end of the summer Lily came back, and Hunter's words echoed in my mind. Perhaps she liked me! I didn't have the courage to ask her out yet, and school was starting soon, but during school I plucked up my courage and asked her out.

Sophomore year, probably the second-best year of high school. At least it was for me. I got much closer to Lily, made it on honor roll, maybe did some typical stupid teenage things, and I went on my first date. I also didn't get shackled to the wall at all, which made me naively believe that my torture at the hands of my parents was over.

My first date with Lily was incredible! I was staying at Hunter's house at the time, and I took her out to dinner at our favorite restaurant and we went to a movie. For the life of me I can't remember what that movie was, but I remember really enjoying her company and treating this time as a date.

Once we ate and saw our movie, I got my first kiss from her! (Well, technically, it was my second kiss with her, but the first one where I got to fully participate.) Boy, that was something, and I'll never forget it either. Hunter was right: Lily and I hit it off great as lovers. Now moving past that first date, we went out quite a bit during sophomore year.

Our second date was a lovely time. We went to a high school football game. I didn't care too much, but Lily wanted to go, so we went. We talked for a while and enjoyed the game. I bought us some sodas and hot dogs, and to this day they were the best I have ever had. Maybe it was because I was with her, but bar none, they were very delicious. After the game we kissed, and I took her home. After that, Hunter came and picked me up and took me back to his house.

Our third date was exponentially better. It was during December, if I remember it right, and we went out for hot chocolate and scones. Though I still don't really understand what a scone is, or why they're called scones. But we got them. We went to our local hot chocolate stand, and from what I hear, we have better hot chocolate in Aslo than Starbucks, and it's not as overpriced either. We sat down on a bench and talked for a while. I don't quite recall the conversation, only that we got closer as both friends and as a couple.

Toward the end of the year, when things were supposed to die down, something miraculous happened. She invited me over and neither of her parents were home. She took me up to her room and closed the door. She then told me, "I want you, John, and no one else. I love you." She then kissed me and asked me, "Do you love me?"

I said, "Absolutely, without a doubt."

She then said, "If you want to have your way with me, go ahead, I'll enjoy it too."

Now right here, I was at a loss. Here my best friend and girlfriend was offering herself up to me! So of course, I said, "Are you sure? If you say yes, I will; if you say no, I won't." And she replied, "On second thought, I'm not ready. I'm sorry I suggested that. If we get married, then definitely."

We then kissed and made out for a while.

I won't go too much into detail about that. It's very personal and private, and, besides, I'm not writing to get pleasure. I'm writing this entire story for release, and I have my doubts in even including this scene in it. That is essentially all that was important sophomore year. Lily and I didn't get separated after that, but I felt guilty that I was doing the most intimate thing with a girl all the while hiding things from her. So, during Christmas break, I took both Hunter and Lily aside and told them everything. Now Hunter already knew a good portion of it, but Lily didn't know a thing. The conversation went something like this.

"Now what I have to tell you, I don't want anyone else to know, ok?"

"All right," Lily and Hunter chorused.

"Now, Hunter already knows this, but my parents have been abusing me since kindergarten. They shackle me to a wall and whip my back. I have no say or choice in the matter, and I want it to end. I really think that you should know, because of our relationship, and I don't really know what to do. No one will believe me, no one believes kids. Also, my parents are the killers of Mr. Hendrickson and Ms. Reid. I'm at a loss. And I really hope this doesn't change anything between us."

"I believe you," Lily said. "And it doesn't change the way I feel about you. I only wish that you had told me sooner. My mother will believe you, and she will help you."

"I don't think she will, and what good is my word versus that of my parents? People will just think I want attention. That I am rebelling because I am, after all, the 'troubled' kid."

"We don't think that at all," Hunter said. He continued, "You have us to back you."

"But what good is that? I don't mean to offend and that means the world to me, but you guys have been my friends forever, and won't people think that we would have cooked this story up?" I remember adding, "I love you both, but I don't want any trouble. I think I'll just endure it until I'm eighteen then I can come live with one of you guys."

"But, the thing is, you don't have to. I have half a mind to go to your parents now and—"

"They'll kill you without a second thought, Lily. I am not going to let that happen to you. I couldn't bear to lose either of you, especially you."

"Then we will have to wait," Hunter said. "I think that for now you should stay away from them as much as possible so they can't do these terrible things to you."

"Hunter's right. Just stay at his house

until we can figure this out. I'm not letting you go back there without a fight," Lily said.

"And you will have to get through me before I let you hurt yourself, John. We care about you, and we want to see you live long, and I think Lily wants you to live long with her."

"He's right you know," Lily said. "I don't want you to die earlier than you should."

"All right, then, I guess I'll do my best to resist from here on out…" I said.

Lily then kissed me and said, "You are one of the bravest and strongest people I know. And I'm sorry this is happening to you, but I've got to go. My mother will be worried about me."

"Let's go, John. We can leave and play videogames if you like," Hunter said.

"Yeah, that's a good idea," I replied.

Chapter 6

Now, allow me to take a break from this and explain a few things that had been going on for some time. A police investigation was launched to discover what happened to Mr. Hendrickson and Ms. Reid, with no success. They had been classified as cold cases, and both were rightfully thought dead. My parents successfully threw off the scent by not being standard serial killers. They used different modus operandi for both kills, they operated well outside of the "five-mile comfort zone" and were not overly involved or overly suspicious inside their community. How I wish I could have aided their search and investigation! But I knew they wouldn't believe me. Besides, nothing ever happens to the wealthy, which my parents were. The police had found a few promising leads. The gloves my father used, he accidently left in Ms. Reid's car, but unfortunately, he wasn't in the system, so he was not a suspect. Also, no one had seen where either of those two lovely people had gone. So no one but I, Hunter, Lily, and my parents knew what had happened to them.

Anyway, my apologies for the digression, but it was necessary. During the spring of my sophomore year, I started cutting myself. Arms and stomach, mostly, to relieve the pain in my head from all the sounds that I heard that triggered headaches from the sound torture I was subject to. As well as in a warped twisted way, I had convinced myself that this would help me build up tolerance to pain and therefore I would be immune to it the next time I went into that nightmarish room. But, alas, it was not to be. The rest of sophomore year was uneventful other than I had to go back to my parents' home for the duration of the year.

Sophomore year ended and, during that summer, I was shackled for nine weeks straight. My father whipped me every day. My back was in shreds. My mother would only clean them once every few days or so, just to ensure that I didn't get an infection. The torture was getting worse. They used loud sounds as they inflicted pain. My mother controlled the volume, and my father would do the whipping. I was then only fed once every two days but given water twice a day. Again, I lost track of time, and I was changed when I came out. I was quieter and more nervous, as well as more submissive to my parents. I only saw Lily and Hunter once each during that entire summer, and that was when my father allowed me to tag along with him on a ride to the store to get groceries or run other errands.

Hunter made me a promise. "I will get you out. My parents are getting me a car second semester junior year. If I have to, I will come and break you out, all right? I promise you that." All I could do was nod.

"And I'll help in any way possible," Lily added.

After this brief conversation, my father came back from his errands and drove me back home.

During my time in that wretched basement, my friends began hatching an escape plan. I only know what I was told after the fact, and I think it best to put it here. Lily was the one who told me about it.

What my friends had planned was the following: When Hunter received his car, and Lily had received her license, they both would, on a Friday night, drive in Hunter's car to my house and liberate me. Either from my room or the basement. Then they would take me to Lily's house. From there Lily would stay with me to ensure my safety, and Hunter would drive to the police station and report everything. From there it would be in the police's hands. And hopefully they would at the very least if not arrest my parents then investigate them.

But I had a long way to go before I was freed from those shackles that bound me. It was that conversation that carried me though the next two weeks of torture. Which was very much the same as I have already stated.

But during that summer the police investigators got a few more pieces of evidence. They finally figured out that my parents were the last two people that saw Ms. Reid alive. But they were nowhere close to questioning them, because coincidentally, and I don't think it was a coincidence, a few things kept the police from investigating my parents. Like "misplaced paperwork", a criminal mastermind passing nearby that was arrested, amongst other things.

Summer passed again into fall, and junior year started. Aslo High only offered three AP classes, two of which were for seniors only. The other, AP Chemistry, was a junior class, and Lily was going into it, so I figured why not? So, I took that class and boy did it whip my tail. I still don't know how I managed to get an A in that class. I remember being able to play with fire during a lab, and there was one rather memorable session.

My arm became exposed and one of the other students saw all the cut marks I had made, and after the period was over ran and informed the counselor that I was cutting and that they were "worried about my safety and wellbeing," yeah right. Like anyone beside Hunter and Lily are worried about that. To this day I don't know who it was, but I recall that conversation with that idiotic counselor with almost perfect clarity. School counselors, I have learned, don't know jack diddly squat. They are entirely unhelpful and really, one has to ask, why do schools waste so much funding on counselors that don't work, as in, the students know better than to confide in a counselor. What happens when you do that or say you're depressed, anxious, suicidal, or have any sort of problem? They suspend you and tell you to get a therapist. Like that's really going to help, and how are most people going to afford a therapist? Why not just lock us up in an institution and throw away the key? That would solve the state's and so many other people's problems, but then there would be a lot of paperwork for the bureaucrats in charge, and that just won't do. So, the kids with mental health issues are just shunted to the side and told to deal with it, even if they are trying to.

The counselor called me in to her office; I think her name was a Mrs. Cavell or something like that.

"I have received a report that you have been cutting," she shuffled some papers, "John. Would you like to confirm or deny that? As well as show me your left arm, please?"

"I can neither confirm nor deny what you have been told, and I don't take too kindly to my day being interrupted by a pointless discussion," I said.

She then replied, very calmly, "Well, I would like to see your left arm, please."

"Why?" I asked. I remember what had happened to me in sixth grade when the whipping marks had been discovered, and then I shouted, "NO! I WILL NOT SHOW YOU ANYTHING AND YOU HAVE NO

RIGHT TO ASK ME TO SHOW YOU WHAT IS COVERED BY MY SHIRT!"

"Calm down, John, I can see that I have upset you, and for that I am sorry. I didn't mean to. And I think it best if you would just tell me what is bothering you. I think that would be a good place to start."

"Nothing is bothering me, except this conversation, and I really would like to get back to class. It's one of the two hours I have with my girlfriend, so I'd like to leave now." I then stood up and began walking toward her office door.

"Now just hold on a minute," she said. "We haven't finished yet. Now I understand your desire to get back to class, but you will not leave this office until you and I have had a deep conversation, or do I need to call your parents?" She then picked up her phone.

"There is no need to call them," I said. "I just don't see what the big deal is and why you care, is all." Much calmer now I continued, "It's your job to care, and I get that, but you really don't. You get several of these cases a day, most likely. And I don't want to be just another file that you have to go through. May I leave now? I am finished discussing everything with you. And I mean no disrespect."

She then sighed, and said, "Show me your arms and you can go."

So I did, and she wasn't the least bit surprised.

"I do have one question though," I said. "Who told on me?"

"Someone concerned for your safety and wellbeing," she replied.

"I highly doubt that," I said. "More like someone trying to get me in trouble."

"Why so paranoid?" she asked.

"I have learned to be. When you go through what I have been through, you'll be paranoid too."

"And what exactly is that, John?"

"Nothing you need to worry nor be concerned about. Thank you for listening, I am sorry for my outburst, and I will be going back to class now."

With that I promptly left her office and returned for the last twelve minutes of class.

When I got back to class, Lily asked me what I had gone to the counselor's office for, and I told her the truth. "For cutting," I whispered. "I'm tired of this pain."

"You don't have to be," she whispered back. "Soon you will be out of that horrible place, and you will be safe with me."

"Can't wait," is all I could say.

The rest of that semester was uneventful, but I had to go home every night, and my door was locked from the outside. I began to stay in the habit of keeping a bag packed that contained most of my clothes, and my most important possessions. Like my iPod, earbuds, teddy bear, and a framed picture of myself, Lily, and Hunter, and another picture of just me and Lily. I don't think my parents suspected a thing, or what was coming.

Chapter 7

Second semester junior year was rather uneventful; the weekends I was shackled and whipped eight or nine times, and the rest of the week I was allowed to recover. I typically was not shackled on Friday nights, which was perfect for the plan that my friends had made. I began to subtly resist by this time. I knew pain, and I was no longer afraid of it as a seventeen-year-old. I still hated pain, and it still shut me down as it does to all humans, but I began to lose my fear of it.

In little ways I began defying my parents. Such as staying out late, making my parents late, and just doing small inconsequential things that eventually ticked them off, but made me feel a whole lot better. I am not entirely helpless, and I did want to get out of there. But how was I going to? Please remember that I didn't know about the plan to get me out until it happened.

I remember when Hunter got his car at school, he was so happy. He got a very nice 2000 BMW Roadster. He took that thing everywhere. Even if it was in walking distance, he drove. But who could blame him? I would have too, if I had had a car. But unfortunately, my parents didn't see the need for me to have one. They also wanted to keep tabs on me, so knowing all this, I wasn't going to ever get a car while under their watch.

I also didn't have a cell phone. My parents didn't see the need for me to have one, and I wasn't fortunate enough to receive an allowance either. My freedoms and options were very limited. Another thing that bothered my parents was me giving my home address to people. Now, when Hunter got his car, he asked me for my home address, and I gave it to him no questions asked. I was later to find out about the escape plan, and that was why he had asked. Now in all this, Lily got her license to drive but not a car. Her parents didn't want her to have one until she was eighteen, which is perfectly understandable, unlike mine. She was fortunate enough to get a weekly allowance, and as such, she paid for most of our dates. I wasn't allowed to have a job, because that would have given me freedom and a way to a means of escape or freedom from my parents. The reasoning my parents gave me at the time was to say, "Oh, we want you to focus on school," or, "We'll pay for everything you need," or, "You're father doesn't want to drive that far twice, and we won't let you be out that late."

While I was staying at Hunter's house his parents gave me money to do things, and that was how I paid for the first date. Additionally, I would always save some back so I could eventually get out of my parents' house.

But now to a more interesting part of the story: my escape and freedom from those horrible people who had the audacity to claim to be my parents. It started out the week after our spring break. Hunter was dropping hints that he was up to something, and obviously Lily was in on it too. Like, "Be ready Friday night. Make sure to have a bag packed." Or Lily said things like, "Are you ready for Friday?" and "Make sure you're in your bedroom on Friday, if you can, ok?"

Hunter also asked me the layout of my house. As well as the schedule of my parents on a typical Friday night. I told him everything he wanted to know, and I began to piece together what my friends were going to attempt to do. I, of course, attempted to dissuade them from their present course, saying things like, "We'll be caught and you two could get hurt," or "I don't want to be the pessimist, but I don't think this is a good idea." To which their replies were, "Don't worry about us, we can take care of ourselves. It's you we're worried about." And, "We'll take that chance, and of course it's a good idea, it gets you out of harm's way."

So, come that Friday evening, my father happened to be out and about doing something that I still don't know to this day, but he wasn't home for the first few minutes of our escape. Hunter and Lily both came in his roadster and then walked in a big arc from the road to my house, which is about a quarter mile, and came to my window.

Lily got a branch from nearby that was three or four feet long, and Hunter hoisted her up so she could reach my window with that branch. She proceeded to knock on the window, which got my attention. She smiled and waved at me, and when I opened the window she said, "Come on! Grab your stuff. We're getting you out of here!"

"Okay!" I said. Relief flooding through me, and a brand-new feeling that I never had before but now felt for the first time: hope. And what a glorious feeling that was! I had hope to never be tortured again. To not be whipped or chained or sounded or anything else happening to me, ever again. I happily tossed her my bag, which she then dropped to Hunter, who put it on the ground.

Hunter then helped Lily down. "Jump!" he shouted. "I'll break your fall, then we got to hightail it to the road before your dad gets back and happens to see my car. I don't want to think about what he will do…"

So, trusting my friend and getting out my window, I then jumped the twelve or so feet down below and landed in Hunter's waiting arms. He didn't completely break my fall, however; I landed wrong on my left ankle and my back opened up as I landed. "Yeouch!" I shouted as quietly as I could.

"You good?" Hunter asked.

"I'll be fine," I said. "Just need to walk it off."

"Okay, we can go slowly," he said.

"John," Lily said, "your back is bleeding, a lot."

"I know, but don't worry about it," I said through gritted teeth. "Let's just get to Hunter's car."

"All right," she said and gave me a quick peck on the mouth.

"Now's not the time for that," Hunter said. "You can do that in the car, just let's get going, ok?"

"All right," said Lily, blushing.

We began the tedious and arduous trek towards Hunter's car. It would have been no problem if I hadn't sprained my ankle, and I was heavily leaning on Hunter the entire way. We were about three quarters the way to his car when my father pulled into the driveway and parked his car. He saw us, and yelled at me, "*What are you doing?*"

"Enjoying my freedom and getting away from you!" I shouted.

"Come back, John! I am only giving you this one chance. Come back *now*!" he shouted angrily.

"Never! I would rather *die* than go back to you! I am never going into that basement again!" I said.

"That can be arranged, buddy!" my father yelled, and he went into the house.

We were about fifty feet from the car when we heard a loud crack and a bullet whizzed by us and hit a nearby tree.

"That was a warning shot!" my father yelled. "Now come back before I shoot again!"

By this time, we had nearly made it to the car, and Hunter was helping me in.

Lily got into the driver seat and Hunter got me set up in the back, and he turned to my father and yelled, "We are never coming back, and you can't make us! You will *never* hurt John again!" With that he turned around and was just about to get in the car when we heard another loud rapport from the gun, and Hunter went flying forward, blood frothing at the mouth and a big bloody spot in his back.

"NOOOO!" Lily and I screamed together. Lily began to cry immediately, and I tried to get out of the car, but my ankle wouldn't let me.

"Go," Hunter gasped. "Leave me. Get out of here while you can." He gave Lily the keys with the last of his strength. "Don't worry…about…me…get…out…of…here… get the police…go…"

Lily was screaming and I was in shock.

Hunter gasped and turned around, shut the door, and was shot by my father again. His chest became a horrible, bloody mess. I knew immediately he was gone, and I hated to leave his body, but I told Lily, "Go, get us out of here. We will get his body later."

So, she drove us the horrible and tear-filled drive to her house. To this day, it was the longest forty minutes I've ever felt.

Eventually we got to the Mansfields' home, and Lily helped me to the couch. Mrs. Mansfield was fortunately at home, and through fits of tears she told her mother everything. I was just sitting there shocked and stunned. I didn't say anything, just sat there with a throbbing ankle. I couldn't believe that Hunter, my confidant and one of my best friends, was gone.

After she had the story from Lily, Mrs. Mansfield called the police and reported the shooting and child abuse. I heard that a unit was dispatched to my home and to the Mansfields' residence.

The police officers that arrived were very understanding and extremely nice to both Lily and me. They got her story and they managed to coax mine out of me. After

I told my story I just started bawling. I cried and cried. I also told the officers what I knew about Mr. Hendrickson's and Ms. Reid's murders and disappearances.

After all this, Lily convinced me to show them my back, wrists, and ankles. Once I did, both officers' faces rankled with anger, and they radioed to their partners out at my house to arrest my parents with extreme prejudice. They gladly complied, but I learned later that the police didn't arrive until my parents were long gone. They did however find the basement and the torture cell, as well as in my father's haste he forgot to hide the crates and the police found several bodies in various stages of decomposition and pieces. As well as Hunter's chopped up body.

A few weeks later, after Hunter was buried, the house canvased, all useful evidence compiled, and a fruitless search for my parents in the entirety of the Pennsylvania panhandle, Lily and I were both sent to Whispering Pine Heights Institute. Where I am now writing this. We were told that Lily would suffer some effects from watching someone, especially a friend, die in front of her, and the doctors wanted to study me for any malign effect from my series of punishments and tortures, which there definitely is and likely continue to be for the rest of my life.

Chapter .8

It had been eight weeks since Hunter's death. Lily walked into the room and wrapped her arms around me.

"Finished?" she asked.

"Yes," I replied. "Finally. Now, what did you discover that you needed to show me?"

"It's in one of the doctors' offices. It's files on each of us and our parents. As well as Hunter," she replied.

"Show me." I followed her out of my room. She led me down the long hallway, turned left then right, and we came to the office hallway, which is toward the back of the building, if my memory of the building served me.

We entered Dr. Reykjavik's office. He had accidentally left a file cabinet open that had our names on it. I went over to take a look and saw files on each of us. I then heard footsteps coming, and Lily and I couldn't do anything to close the door, and there was nowhere to hide.

Another doctor came down the hall, and he saw us in the office. He turned, and by his name badge it was Dr. Goldin. One of the doctors assigned to me. I sighed with relief, knowing we weren't going to get into trouble, after all Dr. Goldin was a nice guy, and I truly believed he cared about me.

He entered the office. "What are you two doing in here? I thought you had a book to write, John," he said.

"I finished it, and it's ready for you to read," I said. "But can you explain these?" I handed him all of our files, including Hunter's, my parents, and all the others.

"Did you look at these?"

"Not yet," Lily said.

"Well," he began. "There really is no telling you this easily, and I—we, as in the other doctors—hoped you would not have found out, especially this way. But you were test subjects in an experiment. Really to test the effects of torture on the human body, psychological effects of child abuse, as well as the ultimate aim of this project was to find a cure for PTSD, or post-traumatic stress disorder, of which you have a rather severe case, John. But I am glad I am the one to tell you this, and I will help you as best as I can. Writing out your experience has several uses, and not just to you. They were for a firsthand account of the abuses which would help you resolve the horrible things that happened to you, and it gives us a clear record.

"Now, I would like to tell you that I did not realize and entirely know what this experiment would entail until last year. I was brought on to be a therapist and to evaluate the results. I did not know that they sanctioned child abuse and so much needless death. Your teachers, the entire investigation, Hunter's death, and everything else was carefully planned, thought out, and executed.

"Once you two have fully recovered—and I will speed that process up—I will get you out of here and out of reach of the other doctors who both took this way too far, and will stop at nothing to reach their goal. I can only trust you two, and two of my colleagues. I have been working here for four years, and I can't believe how stupid I am. For someone with four PhDs, I am pretty dumb. Anyway, do you two have any questions? I will answer them to the best of my ability, and I will not lie to you. Also, we need to relocate to my office." He picked up the files and shuts the file cabinet. He then led us out of Dr. Reykjavik's office and to his own, which was just down the hall and across. He also locked the office door behind him.

"Now that you have had a chance to digest that information, what do you have to say?"

"We were *test subjects*!" Lily shouted indignantly. "We didn't even know! Was *anything* real?"

"Your friendships, love for John, and schoolwork were quite real." Dr. Goldin replied. He didn't seem fazed by Lily's shouting, in fact he seemed to expect it. "Now, allow me to continue. Everyone from your parents, John, to every police officer in Aslo knew that it was an experiment; even the town was built for this purpose. Though many wanted to help you, the majority of the panel didn't allow them to. The ones that went against orders were killed. I was not aware until your escape that your parents were psychopaths and serial killers. But I do know that they aren't your real parents, as in birth or biological parents."

"The same goes for you, Lily. None of the children were with their real parents in this experiment. And I am very deeply sorry for what you went through, John, and nothing I say or do will make up for the pain that we inflicted on you."

"Not my parents?" I asked. "Can you help me find my real ones?"

"I can, but I also know that they are dead, your mother died in a car accident, and your father was killed in a back alley. I don't know if any of the other doctors had anything to do with it. But Lily, I hate to break this to you, but I think you appreciate my candor, and yours are gone as well." He said the last part very gently. He continued, "Now for these files, they are your subject files and everything you have been diagnosed with. The other files are detailed accounts of each achievement and failure of each subject. There is a file on everyone in the town."

"They aren't subjects, they're people," I said.

"Quite right, you are," Dr. Goldin said.

"What are your doctorates in?" Lily asked.

"Psychology, psychiatry, neurology, and neuroscience."

"How old are you, and who of the other doctors are like you or with you in your opinions?" she asked.

"I am twenty-seven. The other doctors that I trust are Dr. James and Dr. Godspeed. You can trust them as well. I told them everything once I found out, and we are of like mind. I will say that if you want to leave now, I will help you, but I suggest you stay until you two are completely recovered, which will be anywhere from four to nine more weeks."

"I don't think we want to wait that long," I said. "I think the sooner we leave, the better. Lily, would you like to leave in a week?"

"Sure," she replied. "This is all very unsettling. I hate to think we are orphans now, and what about the Keshertons? Are they still out and about? Are they gunning for us? Are they going to try and kill John?"

"That I do not know, but I do know that the higher ups know. But they won't tell you. They won't even tell me. Now we need to start preparations for your departure. I suggest your ultimate destination be Denver, Colorado. I will help you plan a route, as will Dr. James and Godspeed. Allow me to call them and catch them up to speed on your particular cases."

"I like Dr. James," Lily said. "He seems like a good man, and he is excellent at doing what he does. He has helped me a lot."

Dr. Goldin nodded and picked up his office phone and to call the aforementioned doctors.

About twenty minutes later, they came to his office, and he greeted them.

After the pleasantries were out of the way, Dr. James said, "So we need to get you out, eh? Well that can be arranged. I think the best route is through Canada, and over through that country and down into Montana, then going through Wyoming, and then you're in Colorado."

"I agree," said Dr. Godspeed. "I think it best if we don't inform anyone else of this plan. Also, I need to inform all of you of certain happenings."

"Well, pray tell," said Dr. Goldin.

"Well, I can say that the experiment was a success, and a cure that will help so many people is well on its way, but I hate how we went about it. It is time that this institution was discredited. I believe once you get to safety, you should go public, and all three of us will back you up. This mysterious institution's name is PharmaPsych. I do believe that they have had some questionable activities in the past, and this will put them out of business with many bad people behind bars, right where they belong."

We then heard footsteps coming down the hall, and a door across the hall opening. Dr. James left to see who it was and started talking to them. Another doctor, I assumed.

Dr. Godspeed then left and didn't come back at all.

After about ten more minutes, Dr. Goldin said, "I think it best for you to return to your rooms. Until our next session, then." He stood and smiled, shook my hand then Lily's.

We proceeded to leave and go back to our rooms. After we were some distance from the offices, Lily said, "That's a lot to take in. I wonder if he was actually telling the truth? As well as what will we do when we get to Denver? And why Denver? This isn't making any sense. Not to mention that your parents, or the Kesherton Killers—heh, that's catchy—are after you."

"And possibly you as well," I replied. "I don't know why Denver, but I think they were telling the truth. On one hand, I am glad to help with a cure for PTSD, but I suspect that it will always remain incurable. Also, I don't think that we should worry about Denver when we get there. There is a long road between here and there. And I don't think of them as my parents, just child abusers and killers."

"I understand," she said. "But now I think we should rest and pack up. I think the doctors will take care of everything else."

"I think you're right," I said. "If you don't mind," I began, not unkindly, "I'd like to spend some time alone. I just need to reflect and evaluate this situation, ok?"

"All right," she said. "I still love you." And she kissed me on the cheek, then the lips, and walked away to her room.

I stood there looking like an idiot for who knows how long, then I went to my room and just sat for a while. Eventually, I fell asleep.

Chapter 9

The next week was rather uneventful. It was just more therapy sessions with Dr. Goldin, and the doctors met to help us get out. Dr. Godspeed gave both me and Lily a map of the facility. He also told us to get ready, as we would be leaving on Thursday. He also told us that only Dr. Goldin would be going with us, as Dr. James and Dr. Godspeed would cover for us and Dr. Goldin. That was the plan, anyway.

Thursday arrived, and Lily and I were ready to go. We would be leaving after lights out, after the other doctors had gone home and the "bad" doctors wouldn't be anywhere in the vicinity.

Now, allow me to explain the breakdown of the doctors before I go any further. The way Dr. Goldin explained it to us was that he, Dr. James, and Dr. Godspeed were against the methods used. Even though they fervently wanted a cure for PTSD and other horrible psychological diseases and problems, they disagreed with the other four doctors overseeing the experiment. In order of importance, or rank in the company PharmaPsych, were the following: Dr. Ames, Dr. Reykjavik, Dr. Johnson, and Dr. Elsh, followed by Goldin, James, and Godspeed. I don't know their areas of specialty, or much about them. But I do know that Dr. Reykjavik was a troublemaker, and Dr. Ames was never seen, making it debatable that she even existed. I also know that Dr. Reykjavik did all her dirty work. Dr. Johnson and Elsh were all right as people but had a warped view of the world.

To be honest, I really didn't like them from the start of the treatment. They eventually stopped treating me somewhere around week five. I really couldn't say, having lost all track of time, and only through Dr. Goldin did I even know what day and how long it had been. For me, those eight weeks were a blur and a dredge.

But now it was time for us to leave, and I couldn't wait to get out of this horrible place, and the third worst state in the union. The only redeeming quality is that it voted Republican in the last election and that it has pencils and chocolate.

Anyway, to the interesting part. Our escape.

I was walking back from dinner when I heard Dr. Johnson on his phone, and he was saying, "Yes, ma'am", and "Are you certain?", and then a, "If you are sure that it must be done, then it will be, however much I don't like it." He looked up and saw me, and he seemed kind of guilty. "I am sorry for later this evening, John. But know I do not do it by choice, and it is necessary to be done."

"What is?" I asked.

"A death," is all he said in reply.

I immediately ran to Lily's room and refused to leave her, and I told her what Dr. Johnson had said.

Luckily it wasn't her that was going to die. It was my guess that it was Dr. James or Godspeed, who I was kind of scared for. After about an hour, I went to my room and grabbed my bag, then I returned to Lily's room. After that, Dr. James came and got us and started walking toward a service entrance. "Dr. Goldin is waiting for us once we get there. Here, Lily, the keys to my vehicle and a pass card." He gave those items to her. To me he said, "You are brave, John, and I only wish I could have a little bit of that quality. There needs to be more people like you in this world."

After he finished speaking, Dr. Reykjavik and Dr. Johnson appeared. They stopped their conversation and just stared at us for a moment. Dr. Godspeed arrived just a moment later.

We were at an impasse for about five minutes until Dr. Reykjavik said, "Now what are they doing out here, Dr. James? I think they need to return to their rooms; they haven't been cured yet and are not ready to be released back into the world. We need them to get better as quickly as possible and then we can return them to Aslo."

"They won't be returning to Aslo, and they don't have the desire to either," Dr. Godspeed said, stepping in front of us. "In fact, I think it's time for you two gentlemen to leave."

"We could say the same thing to you, Dr. Godspeed. Now if you please move over," Dr. Johnson said.

"All right," Dr. Godspeed said.

Dr. Johnson reached into his coat and pulled out a gun. "Now, to business," he said.

"We have been given orders to remove Lily Mansfield from the equation and to make sure that John watches her die," Dr. Reykjavik said. "Now, if you would please step forward, Lily, and make this as easy and painless as possible. You will not feel a thing. Just a slight pinch then almost instant bliss. You will be dead before you hit the ground." Dr. Johnson motioned for her to move as he said that.

"No," she said.

"All right," Dr. Reykjavik said, "if you don't move, I will shoot Dr. James instead, then shoot you." He pulled out his own gun. "Now mine isn't as nice as Dr. Johnson's, so I suggest you do as he says."

Lily began to step forward, but I stepped in front of her.

"Oh, how sweet, young love," Dr. Johnson said mockingly.

"Enough wasting time. Let her come forward to her death. I am getting impatient," Reykjavik said with an edge of annoyance creeping into his voice.

"I won't let you kill her," I said. "If you do, I will kill myself and ruin your dastardly experiment."

"All right," Reykjavik said and fired at Dr. James.

Dr. James managed to get out of the way. Simultaneously, Dr. Godspeed pulled out a gun of his own, fired, and hit Dr. Johnson square in the chest.

Before he collapsed to the floor dead, he got one shot off that struck Dr. Godspeed in the arm. But luckily it didn't penetrate his coat, as it wasn't an actual bullet, just a needle with a syringe that would be released in the bloodstream filled with some kind of poison.

Dr. Reykjavik ran away, disappearing down a side hall.

Dr. James hurried us toward the service entrance. Dr. Godspeed covered us from the rear as we made our way through the facility.

Eventually we got to the service entrance without any more incidents. But by now security guards and orderlies had been dispatched to look for us. A few came by us and drew their weapons but were shot by Dr. Godspeed before they could do anything. I stayed next to Lily like glue; I wasn't going to let harm come anywhere near her.

Dr. Goldin was waiting for us, and he told all of us, "My office was bugged, that's how they found out about our plan. Even though that is bad news and requires some changes to it, I have some good news. A few of the guards share our point of view and will help us, as well as if we leave in the next few minutes. The way should be clear."

"Good to know," Dr. James began, and a crack like thunder was heard. He started coughing and spluttering blood. Then he fell to the floor, as if in slow motion, and he was gone.

"Go!" Dr. Godspeed said as he started returning fire. All this noise as we left brought guards and orderlies to the scene. They also got involved, and it became a massive shootout. The ones that were helping us managed to get the upper hand and drive Dr. Reykjavik into retreat as we left.

Dr. Goldin rushed us to Dr. James's car and got in, as did we. Lily handed him the key, and we started driving off. A few shots were fired at us, but they didn't get close, except for one, which took off the right mirror.

As we left the facility, I looked back. There were only a few of the orderlies and guards left fighting for us, and then I saw Dr. Godspeed go on a rampage—nothing else will describe it. He saved us, I'm certain of that, but he killed like eight people then reloaded under cover fire, then he came face to face with Reykjavik who put a gun to his head and fired.

What he didn't see was that Dr. Godspeed had his gun at his gut and fired at the same time. Both died simultaneously, and I shouted as Dr. Godspeed fell to the ground. Our greatest defender by far had fallen.

The remaining guards shot it out, and it wasn't clear who the victor was. Both sides were in retreat by that point. But the good thing was that no one was pursuing us.

I will never forget that night, and I will never forget the doctors who helped us escape, and I hope most of the guards and orderlies survived. I don't even want to think about the other patients in that facility. Especially the ones sensitive to noise, loud sounds, and whatever else. That's going to be a nasty situation.

Dr. Goldin kept driving into the night and got us as far away as he could. He eventually had to stop for gas, and when he did, he asked us, "Where do you two want to go? I'll take you anywhere you want, so long as it is in the United States."

"Denver is fine with me," Lily said.

"And me as well," I said.

"Denver it is," he agreed.

Chapter 10

Instead of heading north like the original plan, Dr. Goldin went south. He drove all the way down to Winston-Salem, North Carolina, via I-79 and 64. He and Lily traded turns driving, and I just slept and watched the road go by or listened to my music. From Winston-Salem he turned west and took us straight toward Denver. He took stops in Ashville, North Carolina, and then in Knoxville, Tennessee. From there we continued west toward Nashville. Then we kept going west. We eventually got to Memphis, Tennessee, then we drove the breadth of Arkansas and got to Fort Smith.

During the journey we talked as well, and Dr. Goldin told us that Dr. Elsh had been dispatched to kill him, but he had killed him first. They had had a small but silent firefight in his office. That was how he knew to look for bugs, and he thought that Doctors Reykjavik and Johnson must have seen the body and that was why they acted so quickly. We learned quite a bit about Dr. Goldin, and I had severely underestimated him and realized that he truly did care about us. One of the few people to ever do so. I also felt bad at how I shorted Dr. James and Dr. Godspeed after all they had done for us.

After that stop we drove cross Oklahoma and turned north in Oklahoma City. After about three hours we arrived in Wichita, Kansas. And this is where trouble began.

My parents, or fake parents as they should be called, caught up to us. The Kesherton Killers, as Lily had dubbed them, had finally found us. It was actually a chance meeting. We had both decided to stop at a QuikTrip in Wichita and my father saw me in the back of the car. He immediately drew his gun and tried to fire at me. But then he saw Lily and Dr. Goldin and opened fire in our direction, missing all of us.

Dr. Goldin then drew his weapon and returned fire. Lily and I took cover behind the car. Mrs. Kesherton came out of the store and saw what was happening, managed to somehow get to her car and drew another gun out and started firing at Dr. Goldin.

"We've got to help him!" Lily shouted over the din.

"I know!" I shouted back.

The crowd at the gas station was cowering inside while the shots rang out, and I could hear a siren in the distance. Someone must have called the police. Real police, not fake police like in Aslo. I was looking forward to Kansas justice being served.

"I have an idea!" I shouted to Lily.

"What is it?!" she asked.

"Just stay here ok?" I yelled as I stood up and dashed to cover behind another car. The Keshertons were too focused on Dr. Goldin to notice me, but he did.

"John, no!" Lily shouted.

I waved my arms and shouted abuse at the Keshertons. They finally took notice of me, and my mother in her rage, stood up and aimed right for my chest.

Before she could fire, she became a bloody mess. Thanks to Dr. Goldin. Then Dr. Goldin advanced and soon both he and Mr. Kesherton were out of ammo. I ran up to Mr. Kesherton and hit him as hard as I could in the groin, which grounded him and gave Dr. Goldin a chance to recover and reload. After he reloaded, he shot Mr. Kesherton.

"Good," I said. "Now I will never be tormented by them again."

"That's right, John. But now we need to go."

"Quite right you are," I said.

We loaded up in the car and began the uneventful final seven hours to Denver.

When we finally arrived in Denver, Dr. Goldin immediately got us a two-bedroom apartment and set us up for a long time. He got us food and groceries and gave us a healthy sum of money to keep us going.

"Good luck," he said. "I have some business to attend to in other areas, and I am going back to see if I can take down PharmaPsych from the inside. If either of you ever need any help. Call me."

With heartfelt goodbyes we parted ways.

Lily and I lived happily together for some time, we never had sex or did anything like that, but we did get jobs and take care of ourselves. Eventually I applied for college and got accepted with Dr. Goldin's help. I began to study chemistry in hopes of becoming a scientist. Lily took care of our apartment while I worked and put myself through school.

Eventually we made a nice living and moved to the suburbs, got married, and started a family. We heard no more from Dr. Goldin or anything more about PharmaPsych. We assumed that it had been taken care of and he was all right.

How wrong we were, but that's another story.

All I want to put down is that I am finally happy, really happy, for the first time in my life. I have only a dull ache in my wrists and ankles and my back has stopped bothering me, though it is permanently scarred. I have vowed to never treat my kids that way or ever give them up for whatever reason and I will protect them and Lily with my life if necessary, as a good husband should do.

I am finally free from the shackles that bound me.

Thank you for reading this.

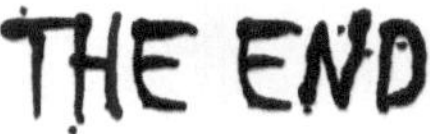